KU-028-335

"And I'm . . . JUNGLE HARRY!" shouted Harry.

But Harry's big sister, Sam, was trying to do her homework. "Can you please be a little more quiet?" she asked.

"Sorry, Sam!" said Harry, picking up his dinosaurs and heading outside to the garden.

They carried on playing outside, but it was a very loud game.

"I can still hear you!" called Sam from indoors.

"What are we going to do?" asked Harry sadly. "We can't play jungle animals quietly."

"I know somewhere we can be as noisy as we like," said Taury.

"DINO WORLD!" everyone shouted.

"One, two, three ... JUMP!" shouted the dinosaurs.
"Hooray!" cried Harry. "I'm on my way to ...

"Dino World!"

"Wow, a real jungle!" cried Harry, as they set off to explore. "Look at all those big trees!"

Playing jungle animals was even better in the Dino World Jungle. Taury practised roaring like a lion, and Steggy and Trike swung about in the trees eating bananas.

"We're just monkeying around," chuckled Steggy.

"Monkeying around! Monkeying around!" called a little voice.

"Pterence!" everyone groaned. "Stop repeating everything." But it wasn't Pterence they could hear . . .

It was a real parrot! "Hello, hello!" he squawked. Soon he was joined by a slithery snake and a very cheeky monkey. Harry introduced himself and his dinosaur friends, and explained which animals they were pretending to be. Snake, Parrot and Monkey were very impressed by Taury's big ROAR.

Snake, Parrot and Monkey explained that they were busy getting ready for the Great Big Jungle Bash. "We hope you can come!" said Monkey.

Just then, they head an enormous ROOAAARRRRR.

But this time it wasn't Taury!

Snake, Parrot and Monkey ran away, but Harry and his dinosaurs stayed where they were.

"I'm not scared of ANYONE," said Harry bravely.

They listened to the roar.

"Her-ROAAAARRRR-low!"

"He's saying hello!" Harry cried.

"HELLO!"

Out of the bushes came a big, furry lion. "I'm Lesley the Lion!"

"And I'm Harry, and these are my dinosaurs," said Harry.

Lesley was very excited to meet them all, but even more excited to learn that there was going to be a party. "I love parties, but I never get invited," he sighed.

"I think it's because of your loud roar," Harry explained gently. "You scare the other animals away!"

"Yes, I am VERY loud," agreed Lesley. "I wish I could learn to be less noisy."

Harry and the dinosaurs tried to help.

They went to the Dino World Jungle Library and tried reading quietly.

But Lesley burst out laughing. "This book is just so FUNNY!" he giggled.

Then they tried playing
"What's the Time, Jungle Harry?"

"You need to be very quiet to
win this game. You can't make a
sound," warned Harry.
    "Oh, I love to win!" said Lesley.
"So I'd better be very quiet."

But Lesley just couldn't do it!
He kept giggling and letting out
a "ROOOARR!" every time Harry
turned round.

"It's no good," the dinosaurs told Lesley.
"You just aren't a quiet lion."

"You could always
try using my loudspeaker,"
suggested Harry.
"Use it back-to-front.
That way, it will make
your voice quieter."

Harry's idea worked,
and Lesley's voice
sounded tiny. But it
wasn't quite right.
"You just don't sound
like YOU any more!"
said Harry.

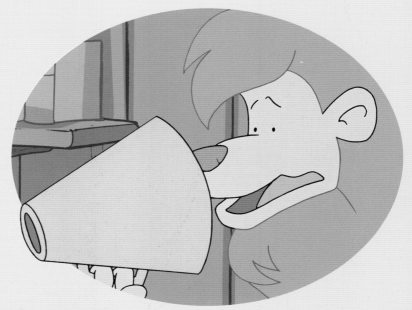

Lesley was very sad.

"I'll never be quiet enough for the other animals," he said.

"I'd better go before the party starts."

"Don't go!" said Harry. "I've got an idea . . ."

"How about coconut-shell earmuffs?"

"Great!" cried Lesley. "Now I can be as noisy as I like."

Harry reassured the animals that Lesley wasn't scary at all, and soon everyone was wearing their earmuffs and ready for the Great Big Jungle Bash.

They all had a wonderful time, dancing under the jungle trees and playing party games. The other animals soon realized that Lesley was a very nice lion after all.

When Harry and his dinosaurs got back home, everyone decided it was time to play a nice quiet game.

"HARRY!" Sam shouted. "I've finished my homework now, so you can carry on with your game."

"Shh! You're being a bit noisy, Sam!" laughed Harry.